OVEREXPOSED

Susan Korman

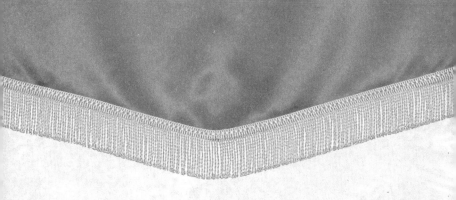

SURVIVING SOUTHSIDE

OVEREXPOSED

SUSAN KORMAN

darbycreek

MINNEAPOLIS

Darby Creek
A division of Lerner Publishing Group, Inc.
241 First Avenue North
Minneapolis, MN 55401 U.S.A.

Website address: www.lernerbooks.com

The images in this book are used with the permission of: © Marie-Reine Mattera/Photononstop/Getty Images, (main image) front cover; © iStockphoto.com/Jill Fromer, (banner background) front cover and throughout interior; © iStockphoto.com/Naphtalina, (brick wall background) front cover and throughout interior.

Main body text set in Janson Text LT Std 55 Roman 12/17.5.
Typeface provided by Adobe Systems.

Library of Congress Cataloging-in-Publication Data

Korman, Susan.
    Overexposed / by Susan Korman.
        pages   cm. — (Surviving Southside)
    ISBN 978–1–4677–0312–3 (lib. bdg. : alk. paper)
    [1. Sexting—Fiction. 2. Dating (Social customs)—Fiction.
3. High schools—Fiction. 4. Schools—Fiction. 5. Mexican
Americans—Fiction.] I. Title.
PZ7.K83693Te 2013
[Fic]—dc23   2012027170

Manufactured in the United States of America
1 – BP – 12/31/12

CHAPTER 1

"Woo-hoo!" said a familiar voice. "Somebody is looking hot today."

I glanced up. My boyfriend, Simon March, stood nearby, at the edge of Laurel King's pool. He was grinning at me as I climbed the pool ladder.

I grinned back at him. "Does that mean you like my new red bikini?"

"Yes, it does," Simon replied. "I like it a lot. In fact"—he moved toward a lounge chair—

"stay there for a second, Daisy. I want to get some photos of you in that thing."

It was a hot spring afternoon, and a bunch of us were hanging out at Laurel's house for a pool party. The school year was winding down, and the party was supposed to be a break from all the projects and tests that teachers were dumping on us. I didn't stress much about grades and schoolwork, but a lot of my friends did.

I let Simon take a few pictures of me, and then I went to dry off.

He kept watching me as I walked over to the table and grabbed my towel. His friends, Deonte Lewis and Mason McFadden, peered over too.

I grinned. "Check this out!" I put a hand on my hip and started strutting up and down the patio like a fashion model on a runway.

"Oh, we're checking it out," Deonte called back.

I put my finger on my tongue and then on my bottom and made a sizzle sound.

"Too bad it's off-limits," Simon said loudly. He came over, put a hand on my shoulder, and kissed the back of my neck.

I turned around and kissed him—a long, slow kiss that lasted until someone clapped near our ears.

"Hey, you two!" Laurel teased us. "My parents are right inside. So let's keep this pool party G-rated."

"Uh, I've got news for you, Laurel," Simon said. "For us, this *is* G-rated!"

A few minutes later, somebody tossed a giant beach ball into the deep end of the pool. Simon and most of the other guys jumped in and started playing keep-away.

"Come on in, Daisy," Simon called.

"Nah," I answered. "I just got out of the water. Maybe in a little while."

I stretched my towel out on a lounge chair and lay down. The pool water had been pretty cold, and the sun felt warm on my skin. I closed my eyes.

"Hey, Daisy." My best friend, Nora Thomas, plopped down at the end of my chair. "That was some show you put on for the boys," she teased.

"Thanks," I laughed. "They seemed to enjoy it."

"Yep. I saw Simon taking lots of pictures."

Nora pulled her long red hair into a loose knot and then started slathering sunscreen over her skin. She has lots of freckles, and she hates that the sun gives her even more of them.

"Oh," she said suddenly. "Did you hear what happened to Alyson and Jordan the other day?"

I shook my head. Alyson and Jordan were seniors at Southside. I didn't know them very well.

"A teacher caught Jordan looking at sexy photos of Alyson on his phone. They both got suspended."

"Bummer," I said.

"Yeah. And I heard Mrs. Núñez might have told the police. I guess ever since those news reports about 'sexting,' you can't look at that kind of thing in school or send it to people. So principals have to get the police involved sometimes."

"That's so stupid," I said.

"I know. But maybe you'd better be a little

careful about what you send to Simon. At school, I mean."

"Yeah . . ." I shrugged. "I guess."

"Do you guys ever send, you know, *pictures* to each other?" Nora asked me.

"Todd and I do it all the time," Laurel blurted out. She was dumping pretzels and chips into colorful plastic bowls on the table. "Since he left for college, I've sent him lots of pictures of myself."

"Do you think he ever shows them to his friends?" asked Nora.

"I doubt it," Laurel replied. "He knows they're private, just for him." She shrugged. "I'm not really worried about it."

She went into the house to put away the snacks while Nora and I lay out on the lounge chairs, listening to the music blaring from a speaker and soaking up more rays.

Bop! I jumped as something bounced onto my stomach.

"What the . . . ?" My eyes flew open. The giant beach ball was rolling around near my lounge chair.

In the pool, Deonte and Mason burst out laughing.

"Hey!" I snapped.

"Oops," Simon called from the deep end. "Sorry about that, Daisy."

I tossed the ball back to him. "Here."

"Thanks." He caught it. Then he swam off as somebody chased him down to the shallow end.

A second later Simon stood up, still holding the ball. This time it was my turn to stare.

Wow, I thought. His shoulders were tanned and muscular. In the sunlight, his eyes looked even bluer than the pool water. I felt a little ripple of excitement rush over me.

Nora was looking at him too. "You know something, Daisy?" she said softly. "That is one good-looking dude you're dating."

"You can say that again." I got up and dropped my sunglasses on the lounge chair. Then I jumped into the pool and swam toward my good-looking boyfriend.

CHAPTER 2

After we'd eaten dinner, we all sat around one of the big round tables on the patio.

"Mrs. Kim told me that her husband really needs a new wheelchair," Eddie Beyer was saying. Mrs. Kim is my chemistry teacher at Southside.

"The new standing ones are really high tech," he explained. "They're made so that people can actually stand while they ride around. If Mr. Kim had one of those, he could go back to work."

"Cool," I said. Mrs. Kim is one of my favorite teachers. Two years ago her husband got into a really bad car accident. Things haven't been easy for their family since then. Mr. Kim is paralyzed and can't walk. He and Mrs. Kim have three little kids.

"Wheelchairs like that cost about twenty thousand dollars," Eddie went on. "There's no way the Kims can afford that. Especially with all the other medical bills they have to pay."

"I wish we could help them," I said.

Everyone looked at me, and I felt my cheeks heat up a little. "We could have a fundraiser," I added. "You know, like a bake sale or something."

Mason laughed. "Uh, we'd have to sell a lot of cookies to raise twenty thousand dollars!"

"So?" I shot back. Mason got on my nerves sometimes. "Every little bit helps."

"She's right," Eddie put in.

Thank you, Eduardo, I thought. Eddie and I have been friends since freshman year. We'd both been stuck in Mr. Andrews's history class. If it hadn't been for Eddie, I might have failed history that year. Or died from extreme boredom.

"Mason does have a point," said Laurel. "A bake sale wouldn't raise much money, maybe only a few hundred dollars."

"So we could have a lot of bake sales," I said.

"There's only one grading period left in the school year," someone said. "That's not much time to raise twenty thousand dollars."

"That's true," I admitted.

Soon the other kids at the table were tossing out more ideas, ways we could raise a lot of money fast—a raffle, a car wash, an all-night volleyball game . . .

Suddenly another idea came to me. "What about a talent show?" I said. "We could have some acts and sell tickets for ten dollars each and have a concession stand. I bet we'd raise a ton of money. And do it fast, too."

Nora raised her hand for a high five. "That's a really good idea, Daisy."

Eddie nodded. "I like it."

"Yeah. It would be really fun," I said. I've been in some of the plays at school, and I like the feeling of being onstage—that thrill that comes from performing.

But Simon was shaking his head. "I'm not doing any talent show," he muttered.

Deonte and Mason shook their heads too.

"No way," said Mason.

"Well, I can play the guitar and sing," Audrey Clark said.

"We know how to do magic tricks," said one of the Shea twins. It might have been Kelly. Or maybe Tara. I have trouble telling them apart sometimes.

"I play the trombone," said Marquise Owens.

Nora grabbed her phone and started taking notes. "The first thing we need to do is get a faculty adviser. I'll take care of that."

"Thanks," I told her. "Between the two of us, I think we can actually get this thing rolling."

"I think so too," Eddie said, flashing me a smile.

"Great idea, Daisy," added a few other kids.

"Thanks." I took a theatrical little bow. Then I glanced at Simon to see if he had noticed all the compliments I was getting. But he wasn't paying any attention to the conversation at the table. Instead he was hunched over his phone, scrolling through the photos of me in my red bikini.

━━ ━━ ━━ ━━ ━━

"Come on, Daisy. Don't go in yet," Simon said.

"I have to go. It's pretty late. My parents probably need my help closing the bodega."

We were parked on the street in front of Garcia's, the small food store that my parents had opened after moving here from Mexico. Through the lit-up windows I could see them and my brother, Raymond, bustling around inside. My mom and dad were wiping counters and wrapping up food. Raymond was sweeping the floor.

I kissed Simon and reached for the truck's door handle again.

"Come on, Daisy. Five more minutes, okay?"

"Okay," I said, giving in. I slid closer to him on the front seat, and he put an arm around me. I closed my eyes, letting him trace my face with his finger.

"You looked really good today," he said softly. "I'm glad I got some pictures of you in that bikini."

"Thanks. Hey, did you hear what happened to Alyson and Jordan?"

I told him about how they'd gotten suspended.

"Well, that was dumb," Simon said.

I looked at him in surprise. "You mean you'd never sext anyone?"

"No, I mean they were dumb for getting caught." He turned my chin toward his face and kissed me. "Maybe you could—"

"Hey, Daisy."

I pulled back from Simon and saw my brother carrying two big trash bags. He was on his way to the Dumpster out back.

"Sorry to interrupt," Raymond called. "But we need your help, Daisy. The store was really busy tonight. Hey, Simon," he added with a nod. "How's it going?"

"Hey," Simon said back.

"I'll be there in a second," I told my brother.

I turned back to Simon. "I really have to go now."

"Okay," he said, keeping a hand on my leg.

"Simon . . ."

He laughed and lifted his hand.

"Thank you," I said. Then I kissed him goodnight and went to help my parents.

CHAPTER 3

On Wednesday, after school, Nora and I held a meeting for anyone who wanted to be in the talent show. Mrs. Frank, one of the music teachers at Southside, had told Nora she'd be our faculty adviser. We met in her classroom.

Nora twirled a finger around her hair as she looked at her phone. "I've been keeping track," she said. "We've got about seven acts so far."

She rattled off what people were doing: playing the guitar, playing the saxophone, two magic acts, a stand-up comedy routine, a juggling act, and a dance routine.

"We need to charge a lot for the tickets," Nora said. "So we'll have to add more acts. I hope we can find more people to participate."

"We will," I said confidently. "Once we start posting on Facebook and sending out e-mails, we'll be fine. Lots of kids will want to be in it."

"Does Mrs. Kim know about the show?" Eddie asked.

"Yep," Nora replied. "Mrs. Frank talked to her about it, and she was thrilled."

"I bet some teachers will participate," Eddie said. He looked at me. "What are you going to do in the show, Daisy?"

"Hmm . . . I'm still trying to decide which talent to pick. I have so many of them."

"You were very entertaining at Laurel's party," Luke Martin said with a grin. "I'm sure plenty of people would enjoy seeing your skill with a red bikini."

Mrs. Frank looked over at us from her desk. "This is a school event, people."

"I'll see what I can do," I whispered to Luke. "But so far I've got two ideas—playing the kazoo or doing a routine with my Hula-Hoop."

"The Hula-Hoop!" Luke and Eddie called out at the same time.

"Definitely!" added Marquise.

"Okay," I said. "Believe it or not, I'm actually really good with a hoop. Right, Nora?"

"Yep." She nodded. "When we were in elementary school, Daisy and I used to hula-hoop all the time. I could barely hoop, but Daisy can do a bunch of tricks."

"Really?" Luke raised an eyebrow. "This act is sounding better and better, Daisy!"

We hung out in the music room for another hour, planning the show and ways to spread the word about it.

Finally, Mrs. Frank looked up at the clock. "We have to wrap up for today, guys. I hope you've made some progress."

"We're definitely getting there," Nora told her.

Eddie came over to me while everybody was grabbing their stuff. "Nora and I are going out for ice cream. Want to come?"

I hesitated. "I told Simon I'd hang out with him this afternoon. He's meeting me here after track practice."

"He could come too," Eddie said.

"Maybe," I answered. "But he's supposed to help me with my math project. It's due on Monday, and I haven't even started yet."

Just then Simon appeared in the doorway. He was carrying a pair of sneakers, and his hair was still wet from the shower.

"Ready?" he asked me.

"Yeah, but . . ." I looked over at Eddie. "Want to go with Eddie and Nora for ice cream?"

Simon frowned a little. "I thought we were going to my house. Don't you want to work on your math project?"

"We could do that after ice cream."

He didn't say anything. But I could tell he didn't want to go.

"Never mind," I told Eddie. "We'd better skip it. I've got too much stuff to do."

CHAPTER 4

"You have a nice house," I told Simon, looking around the Marches' enormous kitchen. Simon and I had been dating since the fall. But I'd only been inside his house once before that day.

Black speckled countertops and gleaming stainless steel appliances lined the kitchen. The family room was nice too, with moss-colored couches arranged around a huge TV on the wall. The first floor was bigger than my family's whole apartment.

A photograph in a silver frame stood on the bookshelves—Simon's older brother. Like Simon, he has blond hair and deep blue eyes.

"Nice picture of Joseph," I said. "My brother says he still talks to him on Facebook sometimes."

"Yeah," Simon said. "He'll be home from college next month. He's got a summer job teaching tennis to little kids."

"Raymond wants to go away to college after he graduates from community college," I said. "He's trying to get a scholarship. But if I go to college too, it will be tough for my parents to afford two tuitions at once."

"I bet," said Simon. I knew he didn't have to worry about anything like that. His mom does something in sales, and his father owns a big plumbing company in Houston.

"Where do you want to go to college?" I asked as he got some sodas. We were about to finish our junior year, so everybody would be applying to schools in the fall. I didn't know what I wanted to do yet. But I was pretty sure I was just going to work for a year.

"I'm applying to a bunch of schools with good communications programs. You know how I want to be a sportscaster or a TV news anchor."

"I can definitely see you on TV." Simon did a lot of media production stuff at school. This year he'd been doing most of the daily announcements that came on during our lunch period. He even hosted a high school sports show that aired on one of the local channels.

"My parents really like you," I said suddenly.

He grinned. "Who doesn't?"

"My dad thinks you have a good future," I went on. "Plus, they think you're a good influence on me."

"I am a good influence on you," he said, moving closer.

"Too bad you're not participating in the talent show," I teased him.

He looked annoyed. "Come on, Daisy. Give me a break, okay? I've got a lot of other things going on—track, TV stuff, AP exams . . ." He looked at me. "Is this going to be a problem?"

"Um . . . " I reached up and put both arms around his neck. "It's not really a problem. But maybe I can find a way to change your mind."

His expression softened. "You can try," he said. "But let me warn you: you're going to have to work really, really hard at it."

"How's this?" I said and kissed him slowly.

"Not bad," he said. "But I'm afraid you'll have to do better than that."

I grinned. "In that case I'd better take a break for now and get started on my math project."

Simon sighed, but he was still smiling. "I guess you'd better tell me what you're having trouble with."

We sat on one of the long couches in the family room while I explained the Algebra II project. Simon was taking Honors Calculus, so he had to think back to when he'd been in my class.

As I talked, Simon ran his fingers along the inside of my wrist. Then he lifted the wrist and kissed it. "You're so pretty, Daisy."

I blushed a little. "Thanks."

"Now I've got a special 'Daisy' folder on my phone," Simon went on. "For those red bikini photos."

"That's a little creepy!" I teased him.

He laughed. "Can I help it if I like looking at my hot girlfriend? And now I can look whenever I want." He stroked my wrist again. "And, you know, if you ever want to send me something better . . ."

"Hmm . . . What do you mean, 'better'?" I asked.

He didn't answer right away. Instead he gently pushed me backwards so I was lying down on the soft couch with him on top of me.

"The red bikini photos are a good start. But a photo without the bikini top would be even better."

"Oh," I said lightly. "I see."

"You are so beautiful," he told me again. His hand traveled up my shirt and rested on my stomach. Suddenly he was kissing me all over. On my face, my earlobes, my neck, my—

"Simon?" his mother called out.

"Crap!" I whispered. "Your mom's home!" I rolled away from him and sat up fast. So did Simon.

Mrs. March walked into the room, carrying some bags of groceries. "There you are."

Simon smoothed his hair. "Hey, Mom. How's it going?"

"Fine," she answered. "I—oh." She'd spotted me. "Daisy's here."

"Hi, Mrs. March," I mumbled. "How are you?"

"I was just helping Daisy with her math project," Simon put in. "She's got this big thing due for Algebra II."

"Mmm-hmm . . . ," his mom replied, glancing around.

She's probably checking to see if there are actually any books in here, I thought.

My math packet had spilled onto the floor. But luckily my textbook was sitting in view. She went back into the kitchen and started unpacking the food. My face felt hot, and I had a feeling that my hair looked messy and suspicious. Suddenly all I wanted to do was get out of there.

"I'd better go," I said.

Simon offered to drive me, but I shook my head and texted Raymond for a ride. Then I grabbed my books and stuffed them into my backpack.

"I'll wait outside for my brother," I said.

Mrs. March called bye to me as we headed toward the front door.

"See you, Mrs. March. Thanks."

In the front hallway I checked to make sure Simon's mother couldn't see us. Then I stood on my tiptoes to give him a quick kiss on the cheek.

But Simon wrapped his arms around me tightly. "Bad timing, huh?" he whispered.

"Simon . . ." I murmured. "Your mom . . ."

"It's okay," he whispered. "She doesn't care."

"Uh, I think she might," I said, pulling away from him.

Just then my phone buzzed. "Raymond's here. I'll see you at school tomorrow."

"Yep. Hey—send me that photo later, yeah?"

"Okay." I nodded and reached for the doorknob.

"Promise?" he said.

I heard a car horn beep twice outside.

"Daisy!" Simon's mother yelled. "Your ride is here!"

"Promise," I blurted out. And then I bolted for the door.

CHAPTER 5

That night I grabbed my brother's laptop and took it to my room. Simon and I had made no progress on my math project, so I had a lot of homework to take care of. But first I wanted to post something about the talent show on Facebook. I logged on and started typing: *Calling All Talented Southside Students! Show off your talent at Southside's first talent show. All profits will be used to help Mrs. Kim's husband buy a new wheelchair.*

I read it over. That seemed pretty good. Suddenly my message box dinged.

What's up? It was Nora.

Hey! I wrote back. *I was just about to post something about the talent show. How was Frosty Treats?*

Good. There was a pause while she typed some more. *So did you get any . . . um . . . studying done?*

Ha ha . . . We were really studying!

I could picture Nora grinning at me.

I guess your project is almost done then, she typed.

Yep. Just have to read everything over one more time.

Yeah right, she replied. *Good luck with starting it, Daisy! See you tomorrow!*

I reread my announcement about the talent show, fixed a typo, then posted it. I was about to log out when my wall began filling up with replies.

Nick Forrest: *I'll do some stand-up comedy. (I make you laugh in English, right?)*

Eternity Tally: *I can do a hip-hop routine.*

Ella Lopez: *I can make some posters for the hallways and cafeteria.*

Some other kids just thanked me:

Thanks for doing this for Mrs. Kim, Daisy!

Awesome idea!

I'll buy lots of tix.

Wow, I thought. *This is going even better than expected.* When the message box popped up again, I was sure Nora had decided to check back in. She was probably excited about all the activity on my wall too.

But it was Simon: *Miss u*

Miss u too, I replied.

Fun afternoon. Too bad my mom came home.

Yeah. And too bad we didn't work on my math at all

We were very busy

:)!

I'll help you tomorrow, I promise, Simon typed.

Aww. Best bf ever!

There was a pause before his next message appeared.

There's a way you can thank me, you know.

I smiled. I knew what was coming next.

Send me a pic?

You have photos of me already!

You promised, Daisy

I laughed out loud. *It wasn't really a promise.*

Oh yes it was!

I just wanted to get out of yr house, I typed.
Your mom wasnt happy I was there.

Well I was happy. And there's only one thing that would make me even happier...

━ ━ ━ ━ ━

A few minutes later, I said goodnight to Simon, got off my Facebook page, and put Raymond's laptop back in the living room.

Back in my room, I pulled out my math packet again. I sighed as I looked at the assignment. I thought I understood the problem and what we were supposed to do. But I had no clue about how to get started.

I just shoved everything back in my backpack. Normally I don't worry too much about my assignments. But the homework packet counted a lot toward our final grade.

If I got a C in math, my parents would not be happy.

Simon said he'd help tomorrow, I reminded myself.

Maybe Simon was right. I had sort of promised him something before I rushed out of his house . . .

I got up from my bed and went over to lock my bedroom door. Then I pulled off my shirt and reached for my phone.

CHAPTER 6

The next morning, I walked downstairs to find Simon at the bodega, chatting with my parents.

"Hey," I said. "What are you doing here?"

"Want a ride to school?" he asked.

"Sure," I said. We started for the door.

"Have a good day, *querida mia*," said my father.

"How's the math packet going?" asked my mother. "You were up late working on it, weren't you?"

"Uh . . ."

My father gave me a stern look. "Your mother and I have told you, Daisy. You need to bring up that grade. No C's!"

"Don't worry, Mr. Garcia," Simon said. "I told Daisy I'd help her this afternoon."

My father looked at my mother, who nodded. Then my father smiled at Simon. "*Gracias*, Simon. Our Daisy is a good girl, but she needs help to stay on the right track."

"No problem," Simon said. He flashed a smile at me. "Right track. We're totally there."

I turned away so my parents wouldn't see me laughing. But outside, I cracked up. "The right track? It's more like the wild side, the way you're acting lately."

"Oh no," he said. "It's the right track." He put an arm around me and pulled me close. "Thanks for sending that pic last night. It's pretty hot."

"You're welcome." We climbed into his silver truck.

"Daisy, I meant what I said to your

parents," he said. "After school we can go to the library or hang out at your apartment. I'll help you with the algebra thing. Don't worry."

"Thanks. I'm not really worried. I just have to get a B on it. My dad totally loves you," I added. "You know just what to say to him."

He grinned. "In case you haven't noticed, I'm very smooth."

"Oh, I've noticed," I said.

— — — — —

I spent the next few afternoons with Simon, working on math. When I handed it in the following Monday, Mr. Greer clutched his chest. "Unbelievable! It's in—and on time!"

"Yep," I said, smiling. "Mission accomplished."

"Good for you," he replied. "Oh, and I saw the posters for the talent show all over the building. So what do you think about my getting up onstage? I could solve some quadratic equations for everybody. That's a talent, right?"

I just looked at him. Mr. Greer has an odd sense of humor sometimes.

He laughed at me. "I'm just kidding, Daisy. I actually don't have any talents, other than teaching math to high school students who don't appreciate my genius. But we all want to support Mrs. Kim. So I'll bring my family to the show and buy a bunch of tickets."

"That sounds great, Mr. Greer. Thanks! See—I appreciate you!"

After class, Simon was waiting for me out in the hallway. I told him that Mr. Greer seemed stunned.

"It was great. He didn't think I'd turn it in on time!"

"He doesn't know you have a very smart boyfriend. I think you'll get a pretty good grade on it," he added. "At *least* a B."

"I'd better get a B!" I said, grabbing him and kissing him on the mouth. I felt really lucky that Simon March was my boyfriend.

━━ ━━ ━━ ━━ ━━

"That was really good!" I called out. Tara and Kelly Shea had just finished showing us their magic act.

On Sunday night, everybody who'd signed up to be in the talent show met at Eddie's house. We were rehearsing—sort of—and trying to get the show organized. By that point, we had about eighteen acts.

A group of cheerleaders headed toward Eddie's back deck, which we were using it as a stage. While they set up, Ella Lopez turned toward me. "What's your act, Daisy?"

I reached behind my chair. "This," I said, holding up the Hula-Hoop I'd had since second grade. It was bright pink and covered with stars and gold glitter.

"Really?" Ella grinned. "You're going to hula-hoop? That's pretty old-school!"

"It might be kind of funny," Audrey Clark said, as if she weren't quite sure about it. "It's definitely different!"

I shrugged. "It's pretty much my only talent. I don't care if I look like an idiot. It's for Mrs. Kim."

After the cheerleaders, it was my turn to show everyone my act.

I carried my hoop up to the deck. Then I found the song I wanted on Eddie's iPod. The beat started off slow, then got faster and faster.

Boom . . . boom . . . boom . . .

As the song built to a frenzy, I dropped the Hula-Hoop over my head and let it fall to the ground. Then slowly I started it spinning around my ankles, sending it higher and higher.

A few people started clapping.

"Whoa, Daisy!" called Luke. "I had no idea. You're pretty good with that thing!"

I grinned back at him, starting to enjoy myself.

I rolled the hoop around my waist, my chest, my neck. In the darkness, the glitter on the hoop sparkled like fireflies.

As the music got faster, I picked up my tempo too, swinging my hips faster and faster. I rolled the hoop around my chest, totally showing off. Then, as I turned toward the house, I saw someone standing on the deck near the sliding doors.

Simon, I realized in surprise. *What's he doing here?*

For a second I thought he had changed his mind and come to help us with the show. Then I saw that his arms were folded against his chest. He was glaring at me. The music continued to play, but the air around us suddenly felt silent and still.

I let the hoop tumble to my feet.

"No!" somebody yelled. "We want more!"

"Hey," I said, going over to Simon. "What's up?"

His voice was cold. "I stopped by the bodega. Your parents told me you were here. I told your dad I would pick you up so he wouldn't have to leave the store."

"Oh," I said. "Cool. Now you can see some of the acts in the show."

"No, thanks." His lips were tight, and he wasn't looking at me. "Are you ready to go?"

Go? What was his problem?

"I'm not ready," I said, shaking my head. "We're still rehearsing, and Nora and I are in charge of everything."

"Hey, Simon." Nora waved to him and came over. "Did you come for a sneak preview?"

"Nope," Simon answered. "We actually have to get going."

"I don't have to go," I said.

"Yeah, you do," Simon snapped at me. "I'm your ride—remember? I told your parents I'd bring you home."

"Yeah. Later," I shot back. "Not now."

Nora looked mad too. "Last time I checked, Simon, you weren't her keeper," she blurted out.

Simon glared at her. "Thanks, Nora. But this has nothing to do with you."

"It has a lot to do with me," Nora said. "I need Daisy's help."

Simon ignored Nora and grabbed my arm. "Come on, Daisy."

"Let go of me," I said.

He froze. By then everyone in the backyard had started to look at us. Including Eddie's mother, who was watching the scene through the sliding doors.

"Daisy?" she said. "Is everything okay?"

I swallowed. "Yep. Everything's great, Mrs. Beyer."

Simon still had my arm. We were making a scene. "Fine," I mumbled to him. "Let's go."

I reached down to pick up my Hula-Hoop. Then I followed Simon as he led the way through the backyard and out toward the street. My flip-flops made angry slapping sounds along the sidewalk. But I didn't say a word until after we'd climbed into his truck.

"Nora's right!" I burst out. "You're not my keeper! You can't just come over there and tell me to go home."

He stared at me. "You mad that I interrupted your little Hula-Hoop routine? You looked like you were really enjoying yourself up there."

I blinked in surprise. "What do you mean?"

"I mean, it looked like you were giving a peek to every guy in Eddie's backyard!"

I gasped. "I can't believe you just said that."

"Well, I can't believe the way you were acting. But I guess I shouldn't be surprised. Not after the show you put on for Deonte and Mason last weekend at Laurel's."

"I didn't put on a show for Deonte and Mason! You were watching me too! And you thought it was funny!"

"I didn't think it was funny." He started up his truck. "You know something?" he went on. "I think you should forget about hooping in the show."

"What's wrong with you?" I sputtered in anger. "It's just a goofy act! I'm just trying to help Mr. Kim buy a new wheelchair— remember?"

"It didn't look like a goofy act to me," he said in a low voice. "It looked like . . ."

"What?" I demanded.

"Like something else," he finished. "Not something you'd see in a school talent show."

I drew in a sharp breath.

We stopped at a traffic light. I turned toward the window, trying hard not to cry as he went on and on about what a flirt I was, how he'd had no idea that I was like that, how if I kept it up I would regret it . . .

I stopped listening. I'd already gotten the message: he thought I'd been acting like a slut.

The light turned green, and he started driving again. Outside the window, lights and street signs whirled and blurred. My heart was racing, and I could feel anger building inside my chest.

Finally we pulled up in front of the bodega. Before Simon had stopped the car, I flung open the door and hopped outside. Simon yelled something behind me, but I didn't bother to stop and listen.

I just kept going, running away from him.

CHAPTER 7

When I burst into our apartment, Raymond looked up from watching TV and murmured, "Hey."

I waved but didn't stop, heading straight for my room, where I flung myself onto the bed. Hot tears spilled down my cheeks.

Did Simon really think I'd been acting like a slut? Did everyone think that, or was it just him?

In my pocket, my phone buzzed.

Simon.

I was still talking to u when u got out of the car. Don't do that again.

I'll do what I want, I texted back. *You're not my dad!*

I am just watching your back. Dancing like that at the talent show is a bad idea. Trust me. U will regret.

My fingers trembled as I typed: *I'm not dropping out! And if u don't like it or really think I'm a slut then*

I stopped typing, my finger floating above my phone for a second. My mom is always telling me that I had a bad temper. And I could hear her then, as clear as a bell: *You have to learn to control it,* querida, *or it will control you. Count to ten, and the anger will pass.*

But, just as clearly, I heard another voice—Simon's: *It looked like you were giving a peek to every guy in Eddie's backyard!*

... maybe we should just break up, I finished typing.

I still didn't stop to count to ten. I just dropped my finger onto the phone and tapped send.

That night I barely slept. The next morning, my eyes were puffy and my throat felt dry and hoarse.

"What's wrong?" my mother asked me at breakfast. "You look terrible."

"Nothing," I mumbled. "I've got a bad headache."

Simon hadn't replied to my text the night before. I didn't know about that morning. I still hadn't checked my phone.

"Here, Daisy."

My mother handed me two aspirin for my headache. I swallowed them down with some water and then went back to my room to get ready for school. But first I had to find my phone.

It wasn't on my nightstand or on my desk. I kicked at a tangle of dirty clothes on the floor to see if it was buried under there. But the only thing I spotted was an old pink sock that had been missing for weeks.

Finally I just got dressed. Then I started looking for my shoes. When I found them under the bed, I saw the phone too—sitting inside one of my purple Converse. No wonder I hadn't been able to find it.

I looked down to see if there were any new messages. Six of them. My heart skipped a beat when I saw one was from Simon. He'd sent it at 3:32 A.M.

I tapped on the phone to open the message. And a shiver traveled right up my spine.

Consider us broken up then. But you'll be sorry.

CHAPTER 8

I walked to school with a queasy feeling in my stomach. By the time I reached the front doors, the bell was ringing. Then Nora appeared out of nowhere, rushing toward me with a weird look on her face.

"What's up?" I asked.

"Um . . ." She bit her lip. "Did you know Simon sent pictures of you to a bunch of people?"

My heart stopped. "What? What are you talking about?"

"He sent those photos of you in your red bikini to a bunch of people." She lowered her voice. "Plus—"

I covered my face with a hand. "Oh no . . . Please don't tell me . . ."

"Yeah, he sent another one too. He must have been really pissed at you, Daisy."

I felt my legs wobble.

Laurel saw us talking and came over with a worried look in her eyes. "Sorry, Daisy," she murmured. "Simon's a jerk."

I swallowed hard. "Did you see the pictures too?"

"Pretty much everybody got them," she told me. "I think he forwarded the shots to everyone in his contacts list."

"Except for me," I murmured, shaking my head.

Nora put a hand on my arm. "Are you okay?"

I nodded. But by then my whole body was numb.

"Can I see your phone?" I asked Laurel.

She held it out. Slowly, I took the phone and forced myself to look down. The first two pictures showed me in my red bikini. The next was the photo I had sent to Simon later—me without my top on.

I closed my eyes. "How could he do this to me?"

Laurel just kept patting my arm. "It'll be okay, Daisy," she said again and again.

"No," I said, shaking my head. It wasn't going to be okay. Not for a really, really long time.

"What happened after you left Eddie's house?" Nora asked.

"We kept arguing. He was really angry about the way I was hooping."

"He got to Eddie's just as you started," Laurel said. "He was standing on the deck the whole time. I'm sure he noticed the guys looking at you."

"Oh, he noticed," I replied. "And he didn't like it one bit." Tears stung my eyes. "He thinks I was acting like a slut!"

Nora hugged me while Laurel went on about how I was just hula-hooping. "So what if you looked sexy up there? You were just having fun!" A dark look crossed her face. "He's totally full of himself. I think he's jealous of anything you do that doesn't involve him."

"He thinks I should drop out. He said I'll regret being in the show."

"He doesn't know what he's talking about," Laurel murmured.

I walked woodenly into the building with my friends. How many kids had seen those photos? Had any of my teachers seen them? I knew I could get in big trouble. But I didn't want to think about that yet.

Two guys from my history class passed me just then. I saw one nudge the other with his elbow. They both looked over at me and laughed.

My cheeks burned, and tears filled my eyes again. *How am I going to get through the day?* I wondered. *How in the world could Simon do this to me?*

Somehow I managed to make it through my morning classes. But my stomach was churning. My head throbbed. I barely looked at anyone or said anything. Mostly I just concentrated on not throwing up.

I had the same lunch period as Nora and Laurel, and I'd decided to try and find them. But when I stepped into the cafeteria, a group of girls looked up at me and started whispering together.

That was the last straw. I whirled around and rushed for the front doors.

CHAPTER 9

I let myself into my family's apartment through the back door and climbed into bed. My parents were downstairs, working. Lunchtime is their busiest time of the day. I knew they wouldn't notice that I'd come home from school. Anyway, I could tell my mom later that I just wasn't feeling well.

As I lay there, thoughts kept spinning through my brain. How could I fix this? Was there anything I could do?

At the beginning of the school year we'd had an assembly about cyberbullying. A dad whose daughter had committed suicide had talked to us about all the ways kids get harassed online. Then a police officer got up and told us what to do if we became victims.

But I had barely listened to a word the men were saying. Instead, I'd been laughing with Simon the whole time. We'd made fun of the policeman's weird-looking mustache and Mrs. Núñez's short pink skirt. We'd doodled dumb cartoons all over my English notebook. Simon and I weren't dating then, but we were on our way, flirting with each other all the time.

I could kind of remember the cop saying that we should talk to an adult if we felt bullied. He'd talked about sexting, and I was pretty sure he'd told us never to forward any "lewd" pictures of anybody. The best thing to do was delete them right away.

So maybe some kids deleted the photos, I tried to tell myself.

But I knew there would be plenty of kids who had kept them. In fact, they'd probably send them to even more people.

Besides, I kept thinking, my situation didn't really count as cyberbullying, did it? Simon was my boyfriend. So wasn't this just called "a nasty breakup"?

The door to my room creaked open. Our orange cat, Pedro, padded in and meowed when he saw me. Then he hopped up on my bed and curled up beside me.

I wish I were a cat, I thought. Cats didn't have boyfriends, and they didn't have cell phones.

I closed my eyes, but the images from Laurel's phone were haunting me.

What if my parents find out about this? I wondered. *If Dad discovers that I sent naked photos to a boy, he'll totally freak out. He'll ground me until I'm twenty-one!*

Waves of anger washed over me. I sat up and grabbed my phone. Then I pounded out an angry text message to Simon: *What the hell???*

It felt kind of good. I typed out another one. *Can't believe u did that 2 me!!!*

And then a third one.

I hope u r satisfied. U just ruined my life.

After that, Pedro and I napped for the rest of the afternoon.

When I got up later, there were three worried-sounding messages on my phone from Nora, and another, just as worried, from Laurel. But everyone else at Southside— including Simon—was avoiding me that day.

━ ━ ━ ━ ━

"Mi'ija? Sweetheart?" my mother said as she walked upstairs. "Papa and I need you and Raymond to work in the bodega tonight. We have a church dinner. Is that okay? Do you feel okay?"

"Sure," I said, avoiding her gaze. "No problem, Mom. I'll work tonight." I was actually glad to have something to do. I couldn't focus on homework. And after sleeping all afternoon, I didn't feel tired. I just had a headache.

All night long the bodega stayed busy. Raymond and I had just finished clearing out a big crowd when a neighbor, Mrs. Hernandez, came in. She ordered five sandwiches for her family.

"It's too hot to cook today, Daisy," she said in Spanish. "I'll come back for the sandwiches in a little while."

Raymond and I made the sandwiches together. He sliced the rolls and spread mayonnaise on the bread while I piled peppers and lunchmeat on top. I was wrapping everything in white paper when the bell over the door jangled again.

My body went stiff as Deonte and Mason walked in. Behind the counter, I kept my head down, pretending not to see Simon's friends as they headed over to the case filled with cold drinks. They grabbed sodas and then walked over to the racks of snacks near the cash register.

A minute later Mrs. Hernandez came back into the bodega. "*Hola!* I'm back!" she called out to me. "Is everything ready, Daisy?"

Oh no.

Deonte and Mason's heads swiveled toward my end of the counter. Slowly, I put Mrs.

Hernandez's sandwiches in a bag, not looking at the boys. But I could feel their eyes on me as I walked over to the register and took Mrs. Hernandez's money.

A few minutes after she left, Deonte and Mason were ready to pay too. Raymond was in the back, so I had no choice. I had to ring them up.

"Hey, Daisy," Deonte mumbled.

"Hey." I didn't look at them.

"What's up?" Mason handed me a five-dollar bill.

"Nothing." I thrust the change into his hand and then pushed the register drawer shut. "See you around."

Deonte started for the door, but Mason stood waiting for a second. A smile curled at the edges of his mouth.

"You looked pretty hot in that red bikini, Daisy. But you know what? You look even hotter with it off."

He let out a weird-sounding laugh, and I spun away from the counter. The bell jangled loudly as the boys left. My face burned with embarrassment. I grabbed a cutting board and a few onions and got busy chopping.

Raymond had come out of the back room. I could tell he was about to say something to me when a few more customers drifted in.

Chop, chop, chop.

I pushed the knife hard through the white onion, slicing it into thin strips like my mother had taught me to. Tears streamed down my face.

Raymond took care of the customers. Then he came back over to me and stood there. "What's wrong with you?"

"Nothing!" I snapped. "It's the onions! They're making my eyes sting!"

"That kid—what's his name, Mason? I heard him say something to you."

"He was talking about something that happened at school today. He likes some stupid girl."

I kept my head down, hacking furiously at the onion as tears kept burning my eyes. Sometime later, a big group of kids and parents came in from a baseball game.

Raymond walked back to the register to ring up their ice cream and drinks.

I dumped the sliced onions into a stainless steel bin, then walked to the back of the store to wash my hands and put cold water on my stinging eyes.

I had a new worry, one I'd been too upset to think about earlier. Raymond was friends with Joseph March, Simon's older brother.

What if my brother had seen the photos too?

CHAPTER 10

The next day I woke up with a bad cold, so it was no problem to convince my mother that I had to stay home from school. All day long I tried to tell myself that everybody would forget about the photos. That soon the whole thing would blow over.

But I knew I was just kidding myself.

— — — — —

On Wednesday I wanted to stay home again, but I forced myself to go to school. *Sooner or later I have to go back*, I thought. *Might as well get it over with.*

I loaded up my backpack with tissues and cough drops. I got through my first few classes by acting really sick and talking to only a few people.

When I walked into chem that afternoon, Mrs. Kim beamed at me. "Daisy Garcia, you angel!"

"Angel?" I echoed. A few kids snickered as I started to cough.

"Yes, you're an angel!" Mrs. Kim repeated. "This morning Mrs. Frank shared more of your plans for the talent show with me. When I told my husband about everything you kids are doing for us . . ." She got a little choked up. "He was stunned. He couldn't believe it. You don't even know him!"

"We know you, though, Mrs. Kim," I said.

"The talent show is going to be fun, Mrs. Kim," Nora chimed in. "It's not a big deal."

"It's a lot of work," Mrs. Kim said. "And

it's such a caring thing to do. So it's a big deal to *us*. Thank you so much."

For the first time in two days, I actually smiled.

Soon Mrs. Kim began the lesson—a review of the periodic table. When she turned her back to write on the whiteboard, Nora leaned over and whispered, "Mrs. Kim is so excited."

"Yeah, she's adorable."

"We're going to meet again after school today, right?" Nora went on. "What should we do—rehearse and then figure out an order for all the acts?"

I shook my head at her. "I'm dropping out," I mouthed.

Nora's eyes went wide behind her brown glasses. "Daisy!" she hissed. "You can't do that to me!"

"You'll be fine," I told her. But before I could say anything more, Mrs. Kim turned around and started talking again.

━ ━ ━ ━ ━

"Come on, Daisy. You can't drop out of the talent show," Nora moaned. "I need your help. And we need your act.

"The show is still two weeks away," she went on. "Nobody will still be thinking about those pictures by then."

I just gave her a look.

"Okay," she admitted. "But most people at the show will just be thinking about Mr. Kim and getting him a new wheelchair."

"I can't do it. I just can't stand the thought of everyone staring at me."

"But you love to be onstage," she argued. "You love being in the spotlight."

"I used to," I corrected her. "Not anymore."

"But Daisy . . ." She looked as defeated as I felt. "You can't let Simon drive you underground. If you hide for the rest of your life, then he wins."

I pulled out a tissue and blew my stuffed-up nose. "Maybe I can do some stuff behind the scenes, like be the poster person or the ticket-seller or something."

"The posters are hung up already," she reminded me. "And Mrs. Frank and Laurel are in charge of tickets."

I shrugged. "Oh well. Just an idea."

"We need your act." She sighed. "And the whole thing was your idea . . . But I guess I should just let you do what you need to do."

I nodded. "Yes. You should."

A few minutes later, she left for the auditorium and I headed for my locker. The building was almost empty. My footsteps echoed down the long hallway.

I turned down the corridor where my locker was. Standing in the middle of the hall was Simon.

Keep walking, I told myself, forcing my legs to continue moving. Stopped in front of my locker, I didn't bother to look at him—I just dropped my backpack on the floor and started spinning the lock.

"Hey," he said, leaning against the wall. "How's it going?"

Ah-choo! I sneezed, rummaging through my locker.

"Fine. Give me the silent treatment. I don't care."

"What do you want, Simon?" I snapped.

He shrugged.

I looked at him, my voice shaking with rage. "I can't believe what you did with those pictures."

"You were the one who broke up with me."

"I said *maybe* we should break up!" I reminded him. Then I lowered my voice. "That photo was for you—not the entire school!"

"You didn't mind modeling your red bikini for everyone at the pool party!" he shot back. "And you look so good in the topless photo. I just wanted to share it with everyone."

Sparks flared in front of my eyes. Hot, angry sparks.

Count to ten, querida. *Control your anger, or it will control you.*

I made myself speak calmly. "I used to think you were a nice person. But now I think you're just a creep. Please get away from me, okay?"

"Sure. But if you change your mind and want to hang out sometime, just shoot me a text." He smirked. "If you're not too busy practicing your hula act."

I slammed my locker door closed, then swiped at my runny nose with a tissue, hoping Simon didn't think I was crying.

"I'm not performing in the talent show," I said.

"Oh. Hmm." He seemed surprised. "Well, that's probably a good idea. Lots of people will be taking pictures that night. And the last thing you need floating around right now are more embarrassing photos."

CHAPTER 11

I kept to myself for the next few days. Mostly I helped my parents in the bodega and studied a lot.

I stayed off Facebook, and I barely looked at my phone or used the computer. The one afternoon I did go online, it was so I could research jobs in Florida—far, far away from Houston and Southside High.

One more year of high school to get through, I told myself. *Then I'm out of here for good.*

My parents knew something was wrong, but they assumed it was my cold that was bothering me. I let them think that. I kept complaining about my cough and how tired I felt.

One afternoon, I had my books spread across the couch in the living room. I was studying for a math quiz, and there was a problem I couldn't figure out. When Raymond walked by, I asked him how to solve it.

"Thanks," I said after he showed me what to do.

"Sure. So where's Simon been lately?" he asked suddenly.

"Uh . . . He . . . uh . . ." I stuttered in surprise. "He's been busy, I guess."

"I heard he's been busy," Raymond said, scowling.

My heart skipped a beat.

"Are you two still going out?" he asked.

"No," I mumbled, afraid to look at him.

He stood up and went into the kitchen to get a drink of water. "That's what I hear. Actually . . ." He took a long sip and turned his back to me. "I've been hearing lots of things about Simon and you lately."

"That picture," I started to say. "I was stupid. I didn't—"

He held up a hand, cutting me off. Then he grabbed his keys and his sunglasses. "I have to go to class. I'll catch you later."

━━ ━━ ━━ ━━ ━━

That night, I went downstairs to see if my parents needed help in the bodega. It was pouring rain outside, and the store was pretty empty.

"It's okay, Daisy," my father told me. "We're closing pretty soon. Go back upstairs and finish on your homework."

I had started back toward the apartment when I heard somebody coming up the back stairs.

"Daisy?" It was Eddie. He was carrying his sax in one hand and clutching a bouquet of daisies in the other.

"Hey," I said in surprise. "What are you doing here?"

"Your parents said you were up here studying," he said. "Here." He handed me the daisies. "These are for you."

"Oh. Wow. Thanks a lot."

He put down his sax and flashed me a smile. "You're welcome. I thought . . ." He shrugged. "I thought they might cheer you up. I don't know what kind of flowers you like, but daisies seemed like a safe bet."

"Thanks a lot," I repeated. "That's really sweet." I got a vase and filled it with water. "Have a seat."

Eddie dropped down in the big blue armchair, and I sat on the sofa. "I'm from the persuasion committee," he said.

"Huh?"

"It's a subcommittee of the talent show committee," he went on. "It was formed by myself, along with Laurel King, Nora Thomas, and a few others. And our mission is to make sure that Daisy Garcia hula-hoops at the talent show."

I gave him a sad little smile. "Thanks, that's really nice. But I'm not going to perform."

"Why not?"

"Because . . ." I flushed. Wasn't it obvious? "I just don't want everyone looking at me right now."

"I hate to tell you this, Daisy, but . . ." He gave me a rueful smile. "Everyone is already looking at you."

I groaned. "Don't remind me."

"Come on, Daisy," he said. "We miss you."

"I think the persuasion committee sent the wrong guy. That's not enough of a reason, Eduardo."

"Okay, well, how about this: We need you. Nora especially. Same with Mr. Kim."

"I know. I'm letting her down," I said. "But I don't have any other choice. Besides, there are plenty of acts. It's not like it matters if I don't hula-hoop."

"Come on, Daisy. Why won't you do it?"

I was starting to feel impatient. "Don't you get it? If I get up onstage, everybody will stare at me and think of those photos."

"That's not the only thing I'll think about," he said. "I'll think about how we've been friends for like three years, and how you're funny and nice and a little crazy and . . ."

His words trailed off as I started to cry. He came over and sat next to me on the sofa. Soon I was sobbing, and Eddie was rubbing my back. "It'll be okay," he said a few times. Just like Nora and Laurel kept saying to me.

But when? I kept thinking. I thought I knew the answer—*never.*

I think Eddie finally got scared by how hard I was crying. He hopped up and opened his instrument case.

I grabbed some tissues and blew my nose. "What are you doing?"

"Well . . . Since you're not going to be at the talent show, I wanted to play you what I'm performing. It's my favorite song to play on the sax. I don't want you to miss it."

I smiled at that. Eddie liked to perform as much as I did. Or as much I used to like it.

"What are you playing?" I asked him. When we'd rehearsed before, he was still trying to decide.

"It's called 'Baker Street.'"

I leaned back and listened as he started playing. I didn't know the song. But he played it kind of slow and cool, closing his eyes and swaying a little. The notes sounded clear and sweet, and they seemed to sail right through me.

I clapped when it was over. "Wow. That was amazing."

"Thanks," he said. "Look," he added quickly. "I can play lots of songs. Including some faster stuff. So if you want, I could play the music while you do your hula act. That way you wouldn't be alone up there onstage. I'd be up there too."

Tears streamed from my eyes again. That was pretty much the nicest offer anyone had ever made me.

"I don't think I can, Eduardo," I whispered. "I'm too embarrassed . . ."

"The talent show has nothing to do with what happened between you and Simon," he said. "And think about it—what will Mrs. Frank and Mrs. Lee say if you drop out? They'll get all suspicious and ask around— maybe find out about Simon and the photos."

I blinked. I'd never thought about that.

"Besides," he went on, "if you don't hula-hoop, what will people talk about around the water cooler the next day?"

He'd made me laugh again.

"Well, first of all, we have water *fountains* at Southside. And second of all, I don't want anyone there to talk about me ever again."

He nodded. "Got it."

"Anyway, they'll talk about your fantastic performance on the sax," I continued. "And Eternity's hip-hop dance, and Mr. Wood's stand-up comedy routine." I paused. "They probably won't be talking about Marquise's trombone number."

"True."

We both laughed at that.

"Come on, Daisy," Eddie coaxed me again. "We need you. And Mrs. Kim really needs you. Promise me you'll think about it."

He held out his fist, and I bumped it with mine.

"I promise I'll think about it," I said.

But my mind was already made up.

CHAPTER 12

On Friday evening, my friends kept texting me from school while they got ready for the talent show.

Nora: *Help! We need u.*

Laurel: *Missing only one thing—an act with a hula-hoop.*

Eddie: *You left yet?*

I wanted to reply, but what could I tell them?

Sorry I'm an idiot who is letting u down. Or, *Sorry I'm an idiot whose boyfriend is a bigger idiot.*

I tried to think of something more positive—*Break a leg!*

But even that message didn't seem right. So I didn't reply at all.

Around seven o'clock, I decided to head downstairs and help my parents in the bodega. But Raymond suddenly appeared in my room.

"I'll drive you to school," he said.

What was he talking about? "I'm not going to the talent show," I told him.

"C'mon, Daisy. It's important."

"They have plenty of acts," I argued. "They don't need me."

"You said it was your idea," Raymond said. "You can't just run away from everything because of Simon."

I flinched. Before, I'd wondered how much Raymond knew about Simon and me. I realized he knew the whole story.

"I was just going to do a stupid Hula-Hoop routine," I mumbled. "Besides, I told Mom and Dad I'd work tonight."

"They've got it covered. I already told them you're going to the show, and they're cool with it. Now move." He grinned. "It's late."

I stood there helplessly for a minute. I didn't know what to do or how else to argue back. So I nodded. "Okay. I just need a few minutes to change clothes and get my hoop."

Raymond was parked on the street outside the bodega. As we drove toward Southside, I could feel myself growing more and more nervous.

That stage is huge, I thought. And the auditorium would be filled with hundreds of people I knew. Hundreds of people who knew Simon.

Inside my bag, my phone kept buzzing.

I squeezed my eyes shut, trying to clear away all the bad images lit up inside my mind.

Me in a red bikini.

Me not in a red bikini.

People whispering.

Simon glaring.

I kept my eyes shut, and one by one the images seemed to fade away, until all I saw was blackness.

A blank slate, I thought.

We kept driving. And soon I started picturing new images.

Bright white daisies.

Pedro's orange fur.

The blue water in Mexico.

Nora's freckles.

I opened my eyes. Then I fished my cell phone out of my bag so I could text my friends.

On my way.

— — — — —

By the time I got backstage, the first act was almost over. The audience was going crazy as the Shea twins performed their magic tricks. People clapped like mad when Tara pulled a yellow duck from a hat with a fishing pole, and when Kelly tried to make a teacher's money disappear.

As the emcee, Hunter Pyle, announced the next act, I spotted Nora. She was standing near the curtain, holding a clipboard, her glasses sliding down her nose.

Her face lit up when she saw me. "Whew! You're finally here!"

Eddie came over with his sax hanging from his neck strap. He held out his fist for a fist bump. "My offer still stands," he said. "I can always play while you hula-hoop."

"Thanks, Eduardo. But I think I'm okay."

━ ━ ━ ━ ━

Being in school plays has taught me that every audience has its own kind of vibe. And the vibe at our talent show was a very enthusiastic, you-guys-can't-do-anything-wrong type of vibe.

Everyone knew we were trying to help Mrs. Kim, and they cheered and clapped wildly for all the performers. Even Jackie Brando, who sang off-key. And Marquise Owens, when he squawked his way through the trombone piece.

Finally it was my turn to go onstage—the last act of the night. My hands felt clammy, and my legs were weak and rubbery.

Nora got Eddie's iPod and found the right song. Then Hunter announced my act.

"And now, ladies and gentleman, for the final act of the night, the most talented hula-hooper at Southside High School. Let's raise the roof for Daisy Garcia!"

"Bring it on, girl!" somebody yelled as I ran onstage. "Show some moves!"

The music started. I dropped the bright pink hoop over my head and let it fall toward the floor. Then I started it spinning upward, past my ankles, my knees, my hips . . .

Once I heard a guy on TV say something like, "Fake it until you make it."

And right then, that phrase came back to me. After just a few seconds of hearing the crowd cheer me on, I sank into the music. I just did my thing, and the next thing I knew, it was over.

I bowed as everybody clapped for me. I had done it. I had gotten onstage with my Hula-Hoop.

The auditorium lights rose a little, and suddenly I could recognize the people in the front rows. Mr. Kim was there in his wheelchair. Mrs. Kim was next to him, along with their three kids. Everyone was still waving at me and clapping like crazy.

I smiled and bowed again.

From the wings, Nora was waving me offstage. Hunter stepped forward, and I started to move toward Nora. But then something—or someone—caught my eye. In the dim light from the exit sign I could see Simon heading for the door.

And then I saw someone else—my brother, Raymond.

My heart thudded. *What's he doing here?* I wondered. He had dropped me off out front. He'd said he'd come back when I texted him for a ride. *Has Raymond been here the whole time?*

I didn't know. What I did know, though, was that Raymond was hurrying after Simon.

CHAPTER 13

Watching my brother start to run gave me a bad feeling. I headed for the steps instead of the wings, where Nora was waiting. By then all the lights were on and people were starting to leave the auditorium. I slipped through the crowd, weaving my way toward the exit sign.

A bunch of people stopped me to say something about my act.

"Good job, Daisy."

"No idea you could hula-hoop like that!"

"That was pretty cool."

"Thanks," I mumbled, trying to keep my eye on the back of Raymond's head. But it was gone.

Oh no . . .

"Daisy!" Mrs. Kim saw me and grabbed my arm. She pulled me over to meet her husband. "This is Daisy Garcia. She's the girl who had the idea for the talent show. Wasn't the show wonderful?"

"Marvelous," Mr. Kim agreed. "Very entertaining." He bowed toward me. "Thank you, Daisy. Thank you very much."

"It was fun," I said politely. "I'm glad you enjoyed it."

The Kims' words swirled around me like white noise. I would have felt bad brushing them off, but I had to keep moving. Where were Raymond and Simon? What was going on?

Finally, I told the Kims goodnight and pulled out my phone to text Raymond.

Are u ok? Where r u?

No reply.

I burst out into the hallway and looked around. A lot of kids and parents and teachers were milling around, but I didn't see anyone I knew. Then I spotted a senior named Barry who knew Raymond.

"Have you seen my brother?" I called.

"Uh . . . yeah. Yeah, just a second ago," Barry said. "I think he went outside."

I rushed out the front doors and looked toward the parking lot. There was a line of cars pulling out and turning onto the busy road in front of school.

I dashed around the side of the building. Then I heard voices—angry voices—coming from one of the bike racks.

My brother had Simon backed up against a concrete pillar. He was yelling right in Simon's face. "Give me your phone!"

"No way!" Simon spat back.

"Raymond!" I yelled. "Just leave him alone. Forget it. It's over!"

"Not until I get his damn phone!" Raymond said. Simon lunged forward, throwing Raymond off-balance. But Raymond recovered fast and grabbed Simon by the collar of his shirt.

Simon is tall and strong. But my brother is bigger—and right then, he was very angry. Raymond pinned Simon against the school building.

"Daisy!" he shouted. "Here!" He tossed Simon's phone toward me, and it fell in the grass. I scooped it up and then looked for the on switch.

I scrolled through the phone, remembering what Simon had told me.

And now I've got a special 'Daisy' folder on my phone . . . for those red bikini photos.

"It's a little late to delete the pictures, Daisy," Simon muttered. "Just give me my phone. This is stupid."

I tried to ignore him, but I knew he was right. Taking his phone was pointless. I'm sure Raymond knew that too. But I think my brother just wanted to do *something*. He wanted to get back at Simon somehow.

Simon slipped out of Raymond's grip and swung at him. Soon the two of them were

89

wrestling in the grass, grunting loudly.

People began to gather nearby. I heard someone yell out, "Fight!"

"Come on, Raymond!" I pleaded. "We've got the phone. Let's just go."

Then I heard people running toward us. "Hey! Cut it out, boys!"

It was Mrs. Frank and Coach Gannon, the athletic director. They pushed between Raymond and Simon, and Gannon yanked them apart.

"What is going on here?" Gannon shouted. Simon and Raymond both stared down at the ground, sweaty and still breathing heavily.

I froze as Coach Gannon looked from Simon to Raymond. "What's the story, guys?" he asked.

"Explain. Now!" Mrs. Frank added.

Neither of them said a word.

"We're waiting," Coach Gannon said.

I swallowed hard. Then I stepped up to Gannon and handed him Simon's phone. "I can explain how this all started," I said softly. "It's my fault."

CHAPTER 14

I slumped in my chair in the principal's office. Raymond sat on one side of me. Simon was on the other.

Mrs. Núñez had been at the show too. After Coach Gannon filled her in, she had called our parents. We sat waiting for them to arrive.

"*Buenas noches,*" my father mumbled to Mrs. Núñez. "Hello."

"Hello, Principal Núñez," my mother said,

her voice quavering. "I'm very sorry for the trouble tonight."

Mrs. Núñez greeted them and then waved at two empty chairs. My mother sat down, then turned to me, her brown eyes boring into my face.

I looked away. *Wait until she hears the rest of the story*, I thought.

My father kept his eyes on the floor. I was sure that he had had to close the bodega early to come here. He looked nervous and upset.

Tears pricked my eyes. I wiped them away with the back of my hand.

After Simon's parents arrived, Mrs. Núñez ran through the story in a flat tone.

"Apparently, Daisy sent an inappropriate image of herself to Simon. After they had an argument of some sort, Simon sent this image to dozens of people. He did this without Daisy's permission.

"Tonight, during the talent show, Raymond and Simon exchanged some words. Raymond decided it was his job to defend his sister, and a fight broke out on school grounds.

"As I'm sure you're aware," the principal went on, "sending lewd images and disrupting a school activity are violations of school policy. So I'm going to suspend both Daisy and Simon for five days. Raymond, you will not be allowed on school property for at least the rest of the year."

Raymond had been sitting with his chin in his hands. He looked up and nodded.

Mrs. Núñez cleared her throat. "I'm going to have to keep Simon's phone and hand it over to the police. They will do their own investigation."

My stomach lurched. My mother did a quick translation for my father, and I was afraid to look in his direction. But I could see Mrs. March blinking her blue eyes furiously.

"The police?" she echoed. "You can't be serious."

"I'm afraid I am, Mrs. March. It's stated quite clearly in our school district's code of conduct." Mrs. Núñez reached behind her desk for one of those little yellow booklets that we get every year on the first day of school and handed it to Mrs. March.

Simon's mother started leafing through it, then nudged it toward his father. His dad slapped it away.

"I'm not reading that idiotic publication!" he declared. "This is the most ridiculous thing I've ever heard. These are kids we're dealing with, not criminals. I'll call my lawyer first thing tomorrow morning, and we'll get this situation straightened out. Come on, Caroline," he snapped at Mrs. March. "You too, Simon."

But then Mrs. March found the page with the school's sexting policy. Ignoring her husband, she started reading lines from the booklet aloud and asking Mrs. Núñez questions.

"What does this mean—a 'wide distribution of a lewd image without consent . . . the intent to harm another person'? I don't see anything here about the police . . ."

While his mother continued firing questions at Mrs. Núñez, Simon slumped against a metal filing cabinet. His eyes were closed, as if he had a headache.

I finally cast a nervous look at my own parents. My father's face was pale, and he kept rolling a button on his shirt between his fingers. Then I looked at my mother. Her eyes were fixed on mine—again.

"I'm sorry," I mouthed at her, shaking my head. "Sorry, Mom."

She didn't say anything. She just kept staring at me, her brow wrinkled in confusion.

As if she were trying to figure out who I was.

CHAPTER 15

The hardest part about being suspended for five days was being home—around my parents—for all that time. They made me work in the bodega, but they were barely talking to me. And I didn't want to talk to them either.

There was no way to explain why I'd sent that text message to Simon.

He wanted a naked photo of me, Dad!

Everybody sexts their boyfriends, Mom!

So all week we worked side by side—
waiting on customers, preparing food,
sweeping the floor, wiping down counters,
counting money—in near silence.

Someday things will be okay between us, I told
myself. But anytime I looked at my parents,
that day felt far away.

My first day back at school, I got summoned
to Mrs. Núñez's office near the end of the
afternoon. I was glad to see that it was just
me—no Simon.

She pointed to a chair in front of her desk.
"Sit down, Daisy."

I sat.

"Simon got his phone back," she said. "And
the police are finished with their investigation.
You should both consider yourselves lucky that
they concluded nothing criminal happened.
I'll call your parents to let them know."

I let out my breath. *Thank God*, I thought. I
knew my parents were going to be just as relieved.

"The Marches have a good lawyer," the principal went on. "That certainly helped. Still, I hope you learned a lesson. Whenever you text someone, or post something online, it doesn't belong to just you anymore. You lose control of it. Do you understand what I'm saying?"

I forced myself to make eye contact with her. "Yes," I answered. "I know exactly what you're talking about."

"Good," she answered. "There's very little time left in this school year. I strongly suggest that you spend most of it studying for your finals."

I nodded. "I'll do that."

"One more thing . . ." Her expression softened a little bit. "I enjoyed the talent show, and so did Mr. and Mrs. Kim. I'm proud of you kids for trying to help their family."

"Thank you, Mrs. Núñez."

▬ ▬ ▬ ▬ ▬

The next day, I joined Nora and Eddie in the cafeteria and filled them in on my meeting with Mrs. Núñez. They were both glad that I didn't have to worry about the police anymore.

"So now you can move on, Daisy," Eddie said. "Your . . . um, unfortunate incident is over."

"I guess," I said with a shrug. I took a bite of my salad. "I'm just not sure that I can ever—"

Just then the two TV monitors mounted on each side of the lunchroom blinked on. It was time for the daily announcements.

My body stiffened as Simon's face came into focus. He began broadcasting the day's news.

"This afternoon, Chess Club is meeting in the library. Boys' tennis players, please report to the gym at . . ."

I stared up at his face. As always, I noticed his blond hair and bright white teeth. Someday he probably would be a famous sportscaster or a news anchor. But to me he'd become a total stranger. I couldn't believe he'd been my boyfriend only a few weeks earlier.

I listened to him run through the scores from yesterday's athletic events. Then he announced details about the senior prom.

How could you do that to me? I thought for the millionth time. We'd held hands. We'd kissed and done more together. But none of that had stopped Simon from forwarding those photos to hundreds of other people.

According to my parents, you were supposed to forgive people who hurt you. But I wasn't sure I could ever forgive Simon for what he'd done. Because even though Eddie said my "unfortunate incident" was over, it wasn't, really. It would never be over. The topless picture I'd taken of myself was still on lots of people's phones. It was a permanent image—it couldn't be erased.

"Yoo-hoo! Daisy! Is anybody home?"

Nora was knocking gently on my forehead to get my attention.

"I'm sorry." I shook my head. "I was daydreaming."

"No kidding," she told me. "You were on another planet. Anyway, before the announcements came on, you were in the middle of telling of us something."

"Yeah," I started. "I . . ."

I looked up at Simon's face again. "Never mind. I don't want to talk about it anymore."

"Are you sure?" asked Nora.

I nodded. "I'm sure."

"Well, then we've got something to tell you," she said. "We counted our profits from the talent show. And we made a ton of money for Mr. Kim!"

"Yep," Eddie chimed in. "Plus, last week some kids and teachers made more donations. Mrs. Frank got us a check for the Kims, and it's for—"

"Five thousand and fifty-six dollars!" said Nora proudly. "That's a pretty great start."

"Wow!" I said. "We're amazing!"

"Yes, we are," my friends agreed.

"Hey, you guys!" Ella hurried over to our table, holding up her phone. "You have to see these photos."

Oh no. I inhaled sharply.

"They're from the talent show," Ella went on. "Look, Daisy. There you are hula-hooping. And here's a shot of Mr. Kim laughing and clapping for you."

Whew. I let out my breath.

"These are really good pics," said Nora. "Maybe we can even get them in the yearbook. If it's not too late."

I smiled as I looked at myself. My hair was sticking up, and I was making a weird face as I twirled the glittery pink Hula-Hoop around my right arm.

Once I never would have let a picture like this appear in the yearbook. But now the image seemed perfect.

About the Author

Susan Korman is the author of more than thirty books for children and teenagers. She lives in Yardley, Pennsylvania, with her husband and children.